C000186045

The Young Ornithologists' Club, RSPB, The Lodge, Sandy, Beds SG19 2DL.

THE BOY WITH A TOUCAN
IN HIS HEART

This book belongs to

Kathrine Wells

The Young Ornithologists' Club, RSPB, The Lodge, Sandy, Beds SG19 2DL.

CHRISTINA BELL

THE BOY
WITH A TOUCAN
IN HIS HEART

St Paul Publications

Cover and illustrations by James Skillicom

St Paul Publications
Middlegreen, Slough SL3 6BT, United Kingdom

© St Paul Publications UK 1991
ISBN 085439 397 8
Printed by Billings Book Plan, Worcester

St Paul Publications is an activity of the priests and brothers of
the Society of St Paul who proclaim the Gospel through the media
of social communication

Contents

The love song of the world

When children lie in their beds at night and long for sleep which is hiding in dark corners, do they hear the Love Song of the World?

It is the song of the Secret Mother, the mother of our mothers and our mothers' mothers. The Secret Mother is a playful mother who never grows old, who has been singing and dancing since the world began, and who will sing and dance until the end of time. You can hear her if you lie quietly, and close your eyes, and let your spirit smile even if your body is tired and your heart is heavy.

The Secret Mother sings in space where the blue earth spins across the starry floor of heaven, wibble wobbling like a humming top among the spheres. She dances with the planets and sings a lullaby to the moon, and the moon smiles because it knows her. Her laughter scuds across the sky like clouds and shimmers down to earth in raindrops and sunbeams and whispering breezes.

She dances on the mountain tops and her song is a snowfall drifting down to rest on silent peaks. She runs lightfooted from the mountains to the valleys far below in crystal streams and waterfalls, and as she goes she sings the song of the birds and dances with the wildflowers which blush to see her coming.

She leaves the stream and flits across the seashore to the drumbeat of the waves. She plunges in and far below she mouths the wordless music of the deep, where whales call through green spaces in symphonies they learned to play before we found our voice.

She sings with the seasons in songs which are yellow in spring and fragrant in summer, crackling like chestnuts in autumn and whispering a white goodnight to the forests in winter.

She lumbers with polar bears and runs with gazelles on the African plain. She sings to the ripening wheat and plays music in barns where the hens lay their eggs. She skips through the cities to the throb of the traffic and keeps time with her feet to the mechanical drumbeat of factories.

She saves her sweetest song of all for children lying in bed at night, for it is behind the eyelids of dreaming children that she writes tomorrow's song. If children will listen, she'll teach their spirits to move to the music she plays, so that one day all people will dance as the trees and the flowers and the stars and the oceans have always danced to the Love Song of the World.

1

Secret Island

*This story is set on an imaginary island
off the Scottish coast, but there is a Secret
Island in all of us. It is the place of the
past... and of the future.*

Secret Island was a small island off the coast of Scotland. For hundreds of years, the people on the mainland had shown little interest in the island. They thought it an inhospitable place, with its grey rocks looming out of the sea and the lonely call of gulls echoing off the cliff face. It wasn't the sort of place people wanted to visit. In fact, it was so remote and isolated that most people didn't even know it was there.

But to the few hundred people who lived there, Secret Island was home. They loved the green meadows which lay like a carpet over the island. They felt protected by the cliffs which held them high above the churning waters of the ocean. They lived a life which had changed little over the years.

There was no electricity on Secret Island, and there were no motor cars either. The journey to the mainland took two hours by boat, and even in fine weather the sea was treacherous. Not many of the villagers made that journey through choice. They didn't need to. There was a doctor on the island, and a school teacher. There were farmers who kept chickens and cows and grew vegetables. There was a shop and a church and a pub. Generations were born and married and grew old and died without ever leaving the island.

But eventually the young people became curious. Some of them travelled to the mainland to see what they were missing, and some chose to stay there instead of coming back to live on the island. They told their parents that life had changed, the old ways were no longer good enough, there was a better way of living. They wanted to live in houses with electricity and central heating. They wanted to buy clothes and television sets and cars. They wanted to go to university and have careers.

The islanders realized that if all the young people went, their community would not survive. The island would become as it was in the beginning, and the legendary spirit who lived there would sing her lonely song forever with nobody to hear her.

There were several different versions of the legend, but the oldest woman in the village, Grandmother Nellie, was believed to know the most authoritative version. The children of Secret Island loved to gather in her cottage on winter days, and with the darkness gathering outside and the mists rolling in off the sea, they would sit in the glow of her log fire and listen as she recounted the story which she had told more times than anyone could remember.

'Long, long ago,' said Grandmother Nellie, 'there were no people living on the island. It belonged to the gulls, and the otters, and the foxes, but it also belonged to the spirit. They say it used to be called Sacred Island, because of the spirit who lived here.'

The children sat around her feet and looked up at her with cheeks flushed from the fire and eyes bright with anticipation. 'Who was the spirit, Grandmother Nellie?' they asked, although they had heard the story often before.

'The spirit? Ah, if I could answer that question, I would be wiser than the spirit,' smiled Grandmother Nellie, and allowed the silence to stretch out so that the creak of her rocking chair and the crackle of the fire heightened their suspense.

'Can't you guess who the spirit was?' asked the youngest child, unable to wait any longer.

Grandmother Nellie closed her eyes. 'The spirit was a woman. Some say she was a beautiful woman, although few understood her beauty for she was a mysterious spirit, visible only to those who knew where to look.'

'Was she a happy spirit, Grandmother Nellie?'

Grandmother Nellie shook her head and again she allowed a long silence to fill the room before she replied. 'She was a restless spirit. She was looking for someone, and until she found him she could never be truly happy. But she was creative in her sadness. When she cried, her tears were the rain which watered the seeds and filled the meadows with hedgerows and flowers. When she called her lover, her voice filled the air with a strange, melancholic beauty. When she searched about the island, her robe billowed out and spread a white mist over the fields.'

'Did anybody ever come to the island?' asked a boy who knew to ask the questions in their proper order so that the telling of the story would follow its old familiar pattern. Soon he would be too old to be entertained by the story. He would want to join all the other young people who had travelled to the mainland to find a more interesting life.

'Sometimes sailors came on their way to the mainland,' said Grandmother Nellie, 'but they never stayed. They were looking for trade, for people to barter with, for riches to claim. The island offered them none of those things, so they quickly left in search of better places.'

'But one of them stayed, didn't he?'

'Yes, at last a sailor came who was looking for something different. He anchored his boat and climbed up the Hidden Path to the top of the island.'

The children wriggled and drew closer to one another. The Hidden Path was a narrow, slippery passage which wound up in a dark crevasse between the cliff faces. They were forbidden to play there, for a careless step would send them hurtling onto the rocks below.

'When the sailor reached the top, he sat down on the Welcome Stone.'

This too was a familiar landmark to the

children, the smooth rock with comfortable hollows where the fishermen liked to sit after the arduous climb up from their boats.

'He closed his eyes and felt the peace of the island seeping through him. Far below, the waves exploded against the rocks. The wind whispered so that the grass bent and shimmered beneath it. The gulls wheeled above him, white wings spread against the sky.'

She leaned her head against her chair and she might have been asleep were it not for the steady rocking of her chair.

'After a while, the sailor realized that the gulls, the wind, the ocean and the grass were trying to tell him something. He listened intently for many hours, for it was not an easy message to understand but it was a wonderful message, a message he had been sailing the seas to hear.' The children sat quietly, listening as the sailor once listened. 'The wind was singing a love song, caressing his hair with a woman's touch,' said Grandmother Nellie. '"I have been waiting for you forever," sang the wind. The waves were a heartbeat pressed close against his ear. The grass was bending under a hidden footfall, yielding to an unseen presence. The gulls were an expression of joy, soaring up in celebration. "Who are you?" asked the sailor. "My name is Wisdom," the spirit replied. "Where do you come from?" he asked. "I am your own thoughts coming to meet you, your own longings being fulfilled," she answered. The sailor was filled with love for this strange spirit. "Where are you?" he asked. "How can I find you?" "You are with me," she said. "I am the air that you breathe. I am the seasons and the sunshine. I am the colour of the trees and the song of the birds. When you set out to look for me, you had already found me. Before you recognised me, you knew me. I will be with you and your children forever, coming towards you wherever you go."'

'What happened next?' asked a child.

'Nobody really knows,' said Grandmother Nellie, her voice barely rising above the moan of the wind against the shutters. The mists blew in from the ocean like a fine veil falling over the island and the man. Some say he married the woman spirit, and they had children. They say that the man went fishing to feed his children one day, but a storm blew up and he was drowned. The spirit cared for the children and has stayed with them ever since, but she grieves over the death of the man and longs to be reunited with him. That is why the wind still sings a mournful song over the island, and the waves still beat like a lonely heart against the cliffs. She cries for the man as she waits for him to come back, but her tears always bring new growth and fresh buds to the trees.'

The children huddled together around her feet. 'Will the man come back, Grandmother Nellie?'

'Who knows, children, who knows?'

They knew that the story was over. It was

getting dark and their parents were waiting for them. Grandmother Nellie stood on her door-step and waved to them as they set off into the night. She knew that they would be safe, be-cause the spirit had promised never to leave the island children.

But the parents wondered who would pro-tect their children when they grew up and left the island? There were so many dangers, so many terrors away from the loving care of the island spirit.

They held meetings in the church hall and in the pub to discuss the problem of their children. Finally, they agreed on a plan of action. They would write a letter to their Member of Parliament in London. There was some discussion about whether the school teacher or the doctor should write the letter, but in the end they agreed the school teacher should write it. They sat far into the night, telling him what he should say.

They wanted the government to build a bridge, for although the crossing was long and dangerous by sea, it was a distance of only a few miles and the teacher said there were many bridges longer than that in the world. They also wanted electricity to be brought to the island. Then their children could have tel-evisions and central heating. They could travel forwards and backwards by car between the mainland and the island in less than an hour. Even if they moved away, their links with the island would not be broken. And if the way of life was the same on the island as it was in the cities, perhaps they wouldn't be so eager to leave.

Not all of them thought this was a good idea. Fergus the pub keeper thought it would bring trouble to the island, and the Reverend McFife said the islanders would be contaminated by the ways of the world. But eventually the letter was written and sent in the weekly shipment of mail.

The Member of Parliament was sympathetic to the islanders' request. He came to see them, arriving in a helicopter and visiting them in their homes. The arrival of a helicopter was a rare event, seen only in cases of emergency like the time George the fisherman had fallen on the Hidden Path and broken his leg, or when little Rosie McPherson was born too soon and had to be flown to hospital to live in an incubator until she was strong and healthy.

All the villagers did their best to explain their case to the Member of Parliament. None of them was sure of the correct way to address him, so they called him a variety of titles. 'I don't like it, Your Grace,' said Fergus, as the Member of Parliament drank a pint of beer in the pub. 'No, I don't like it at all. First it'll be a bridge, then the tourists will start arriving, then the next thing is I'll have long-haired gits in leather jackets arriving on a Saturday night, wanting juke boxes and video games and those daft red cherries for their girlfriends' drinks. No. I don't like it at all.'

'Oh, your Honourable Excellency, I think it's a wonderful idea,' said Mrs Gillick who lived in the cottage next to Grandmother Nellie's. 'My daughter and my son have left the island,' she said. 'They say it's too primitive and boring here. My daughter's got married and she's got a microwave oven. She can cook a Sunday roast in less than twenty minutes. Marvellous, isn't it? Less than twenty minutes. It's no wonder she doesn't want to live here, out collecting wood on a winter's morning with the icicles forming on the end of your nose to get the stove going before you can bake the bread for the family's breakfast.'

'It will bring sin to the island, Sir,' said Reverend McFife. 'The islanders are good, wholesome people, kept pure from the wickedness of the world. I've seen what happens to our young people when they go to the city. Young Laura Campbell came back here with green hair and a ring through her nose. I said, "Laura Campbell, if the Lord had meant you to have a ring through your nose, you'd have been born a bull."'

Only Grandmother Nellie had no opinion to offer the Member of Parliament. She offered him tea and the finest cake he had ever tasted, but when he asked her what she thought about the bridge she smiled and said she hadn't really thought about it at all.

It took several years to build the bridge. The children watched in excitement as a huge building site took shape on the clifftops, while

Fergus muttered about the noise and the pollution, and Reverend McFife preached sermons warning them against the ways of the world. At last it was finished, and on a blue summer day with a breeze blowing in off the sea, the Queen came to open the bridge. There was a party and people from the mainland came to celebrate. Somebody took a photograph of Grandmother Nellie shaking the Queen's hand, and the picture appeared on the front page of newspapers all over Britain the next day.

With the arrival of cars and electricity, the islanders' lives changed beyond recognition. The island became a popular holiday resort – travel agents advertised it as a trip into the past, an opportunity to escape to an unspoilt world. They built holiday cottages and opened a caravan park in the green field where the sailor had first heard the song of the woman. Somebody thought of putting a brass plaque on the Welcome Stone, telling the legend of the woman spirit and the sailor. The legend became famous, and tourist shops sold souvenirs – plaster sailors and china woman spirits with *Greetings from Secret Island* written across the base. Fergus the pub keeper still grumbled, but he became rich because so many people visited the pub. Reverend McFife still preached against the wicked ways of the world, but people flocked to visit the old stone church and the collection boxes were heavy with their offerings. The islanders gossipped together as they had always done, but now there was only one subject of conversation among them. What had happened to their island? It was now crowded and covered with litter. The people who came from the mainland were very noisy and intrusive. They grumbled and they complained, but over the years they all bought cars, and built new houses because they could sell their old cottages to lawyers and businessmen from London for more money than they had dreamed of earning in a lifetime.

Grandmother Nellie's hair grew as white as the snow which still covered the island in winter and drove the tourists away. She still lived in her cottage without electricity, and the children still gathered on winter nights to hear the legend. When they grew up and went to college and took up careers in the cities, they came back to see her and brought their own children. She never criticised them for having rings through their noses, or for dyeing their hair green, or for wearing leather jackets and torn jeans. She was so well-loved and so well-known that she was almost a legend in her own right. Some people said that she was the only truly unspoilt thing left on the island.

Then one day, everything changed again. There was a terrible storm at sea. A ship was blown off course. The captain said he had lost control and he was going to hit the bridge. Police cleared all the traffic and closed the bridge, and the islanders stood on the cliff tops and watched while the sky churned darkly overhead and lightning sliced through the

clouds. The ship was driven closer and closer to the concrete piers which supported the bridge, until it smashed into one and the central section of the bridge collapsed, dragging down with it into the sea the cables which had brought electricity to the island people.

Once again, the island was cut off from the outside world. There would be no more tourists, no more caravans and people eating hamburgers and chips out of paper bags. Reverend McFife said it was an act of God.

The islanders once more engaged in deep conversation late into the night. With the bridge down, they could recapture the old ways of living. They would be a small community again, growing their own food, running their own school, living a simple, natural life. Reverend McFife was right. It was God who had done this for them. They were children of the woman spirit and the man. They were not like the people who lived on the mainland. Now that they knew what the world was like, they would ban their children from ever leaving the island. They would never let them look at newspapers or listen to the radio or read books which might make them curious about other ways of living. They would keep themselves pure and apart forever.

But then they thought of other things.

'Remember when young Bobby fell on the rocks all those years ago?' said one woman. 'He died because it was too stormy for the helicopter to take him to hospital. If there had been a bridge then, an ambulance would have taken him and he'd have been alive today.'

'I shall miss my record player,' said another. 'I'd never heard Mozart's music until we had electricity.'

'I loved watching television,' said somebody else, 'and seeing all those other places and other people. I didn't know we lived in such a varied and wonderful world.'

'Think of waking up every morning in winter when it's cold and dark, and having no electric lights and no heating in the house.'

'I used to like going to the theatre on a Saturday night.'

'I enjoyed meeting new people every summer. It made life interesting, having so many different types visiting us.'

'I shall have to close my souvenir shop now. I won't have any more customers. The islanders won't want to buy souvenirs, will they?'

'And what will become of the hotel? My husband and I put all our savings into that hotel. What will happen to us now?'

'My daughter has done so well at university. She'll qualify as a doctor next year.'

On and on they went, remembering how many advantages there had been to modern life. Finally, they were so confused that they didn't know whether they wanted the bridge to be repaired or not. The next day, they spoke about their problems to Grandmother Nellie.

'We think the woman spirit would prefer us

to stay as we are, but we've realized that modern life isn't all bad.'

Grandmother Nellie smiled and said nothing.

'The spirit said she'd look after the island children forever. We've gone against her wishes by making it so easy to leave the island. We must go back to our old ways.'

Grandmother Nellie listened intently, but still she was silent.

'We've lost our spirituality, haven't we, Grandmother Nellie?'

Grandmother Nellie seemed to find that funny. Her face crinkled in a soft laugh and her blue eyes sparkled.

'What's the joke, Grandmother Nellie? This is very serious. We need your help. What do you think the island spirit wants us to do?'

'Ah, if I knew that, I would be wiser than the spirit,' said Grandmother Nellie.

'That doesn't help us much, does it? Tell us what we should do.'

'The sailor searched until he found what he was looking for,' said Grandmother Nellie. 'He didn't expect it to be easy. Even when he found it, his search wasn't over. He had to listen to understand the message. You have to recognise your own thoughts coming to meet you. To know what the spirit wants, you must take time to understand her.'

'Who is she, Grandmother Nellie? How can we understand somebody we have never seen?'

'She is the seasons and the sunshine, the

colour of the trees and the song of the birds. Are there no seasons and no birds singing anywhere but on the island? Did the bridge lead to a different world, protected by a different spirit? Her name is Wisdom. You need to recognise her in the fulfilment of your own longings, in the situations to which your longings lead you.'

'You're talking in riddles, Grandmother Nellie,' they said.

'The spirit also talks in riddles. Those who are truly her children understand the riddles.'

Did the islanders repair the bridge? Did they mix with the people from the mainland and listen to the song of the birds in the cities as well as on the island? Did they find Wisdom coming to meet them, whichever road they travelled along? Or did the bridge remain broken forever, a jagged reminder of another way of living which some said was better and others said was worse, taunting the young people of the island with its broken promise of freedom? To know the answer, you'll have to listen to what the wind is telling you.

2

Cecily visits the city

Cecily and Sam lived next door to each other in the city, but when Cecily and her family moved to the country, Sam began to wonder if they could possibly still be friends.

In their fourth year at junior school, Cecily and Sam were the best of friends. They sat at the same table, hated school dinners, loved cold pizzas in their lunch boxes, and thought Mr. Jones, their teacher, was a bore. When Billy pushed Cecily over in the playground, it was Sam who thought of putting a toad in his satchel. When Sam was given detention for putting a toad in Billy's satchel, Cecily stayed in the classroom to keep her company instead of going out to play with the other children.

Cecily and Sam lived next door to each other in a row of terraced houses near the school. Cecily was an only child and she had her own room, but Sam had two brothers and a sister, so she shared a room with her sister.

Cecily and Sam walked to school together every morning, and went home together every evening. During the school holidays, they went shopping together on the bus, went to the cinema together, listened to music together, rode their bikes together.

If all this sounds a bit too good to be true, you're right. They also fought together, and sometimes they shouted so loud that old Mrs Green who lived next door would complain to their mothers.

'Can't you keep those children quiet?' she would grumble. 'When I was a girl, we weren't allowed to speak like that. And the language! I've never heard anything like it.'

Sometimes these fights would last for a whole day, and Sam would tell her mother, 'Cecily isn't my friend any more,' and Cecily would tell her mother, 'I'm never playing with that pig-faced idiot again,' and Cecily's mother would say, 'Really Cecily,' but the next day Sam would ring the doorbell and they would do everything together again until their next fight.

Then one day, Cecily came to collect Sam with red eyes and a blocked nose, and as they walked to school she kept sniffing and wiping her eyes as she told Sam the most terrible news.

'We're moving house. We're going to live in the country. Mum says she doesn't want me growing up in the city. It's too rough, and she doesn't think much of the school either. They've bought a cottage with a big garden, and they're sending me to a private school. They say that I'll get a much healthier upbringing in the country.'

'That's terrible,' gasped Sam. 'What about your friends? I bet they'll sell your house to somebody really gross, and then I'll have nobody to play with.'

As it happened, the people who bought Cecily's house weren't too bad. They had a son called Matthew who was the same age as Sam, and he wasn't bad as boys go. But Sam missed Cecily so much that sometimes she thought her heart would burst with sadness. They wrote to each other every week, and as the school holidays approached Sam got more and more miserable until her mother asked her what was wrong.

'What will I do in the holidays without Cecily? I'll be so bored, and I'll have nobody to play with, and you won't let me go to town on the bus by myself.'

Her mother stroked her hair. 'It's really hard when friends move away. It's part of growing up Sam, to learn to let people go, even people you love very much. But I have an idea. Why don't you invite Cecily to spend a few days with you during the holidays?'

'Can I really? Oh Mum, that's a fantastic idea! D'you think her mother will let her come?'

Cecily's mother did let her go, after she'd spoken on the telephone with Sam's mother for nearly an hour, and written two long letters full of instructions.

The night before Cecily was due to arrive, Sam's mother sat on her bed.

'Sam dear, I know how much you're looking forward to seeing Cecily again, but you need to remember that sometimes people change. This is the first time Cecily has lived anywhere else. Things are different for her now, and ... well, I just want to warn you not to be too disappointed if she's changed.'

Sam nodded because she knew if she argued her mum would give her a lecture, and she wanted to get on with reading her book. But deep down, she was convinced her mum was wrong. Cecily would never change. They would be friends forever and ever.

She woke up the next morning with that wide-awake, happy, summertime feeling inside her. She put on her best jeans – the old ones with torn knees, just like Cecily's. She hoped Cecily would remember to bring her bike. Matthew next door had taught Sam how to skateboard, and he'd said he would teach Cecily too. The holidays were going to be the best ever.

She heard a car stopping outside, and she looked out of the window. It was a shiny new red car, and a girl got out of the passenger door wearing a blue spotted dress and white socks, carrying a white bag with pink ponies on it. With a horrible, wobbly sensation in her stomach, Sam realized it was Cecily. She watched from the top of the stairs as Cecily's mother kissed her goodbye, leaving a red lipstick mark on her cheek.

'You be a good girl, darling, and remember all the things I told you. I don't want you getting into trouble.'

Then nothing in the world mattered except seeing Cecily again, and Sam bounded down the stairs two at a time to say hello to her friend.

The day was a disaster.

Sam had persuaded her mum to give them

cold pizzas for lunch. Cecily looked down at her plate and wrinkled her nose.

'Would it be possible to warm my pizza up, Mrs Coles?' she asked.

Sam's mum got that irritated look on her face when she flared her nostrils and drew down her eyebrows. 'I thought you loved cold pizza,' she said in the kind of voice which made Sam nervous.

'No, I've gone off it. Don't you have a micro-wave? You could just pop it in there for a minute or two.'

'You know we don't have a microwave, Cecily.' Sam hoped her mum would remember Cecily was a guest and be polite to her.

Cecily giggled. 'Oh, I forgot. Where we live, everybody has microwaves.'

'I'll put it under the grill if you like,' said Sam's mum, clattering down her knife and fork a bit too loudly.

'Thanks,' said Cecily, flashing her a pretty smile.

The telephone rang and by the time Sam's mum finished talking, the pizza was frazzled.

'Never mind,' said Cecily daintily. 'I'm not that hungry anyway. I'll just nibble on a stick of celery instead.'

After lunch, Sam asked Cecily if she'd like to go for a ride.

'I haven't brought my bike,' said Cecily.

'I'm sure Matthew next door would let you borrow his,' said Sam.

'I'm not riding a boy's bike! And anyway,

mummy says she doesn't want me riding my bike on the road. She says it's too dangerous.'

'Oh.' Sam wondered what on earth they were going to do for the rest of the afternoon, and then she remembered that Cecily was there for five whole days. She had a little flicker of wishing she hadn't invited her, but that made her feel guilty and disloyal – after all, Cecily was her best friend in the whole world.

'Tell me about your new house and your school,' she said.

'Our house is fantastic. Mummy's done my room with really nice frilly curtains, and I've got a brand new dressing table with all my things arranged on it. I've got a pony too now, and I go riding every Saturday morning. The school is much better than our old school. There are only fifteen people in my class, and we've got lots of new computers, and new books, and the art room is fantastic. Not like here where we had to share books and only got to use the computer once a week. Most of my friends have their own computers anyway. I've got a music centre in my bedroom too. There's a girl in my class with the same name as you, but she doesn't shorten her name. She calls herself Samantha.'

Sam couldn't think of anything to say. 'D'you want to meet my new friend?' she asked after a while. 'His name's Matthew and he lives in your old house.'

Cecily shrugged. 'I don't mind,' she said.

She looked around. 'I can't believe we used to live in a house as small as this,' she said.

Sam looked around too. Small? She'd never thought of her house as being small before. It was the same size as everybody else's round here, except for the ones with loft conversions of course. Her dad had said they might do a loft conversion for her one day, when she was a teenager and wanted her own room.

Cecily didn't seem to approve of Sam's life – she didn't eat cold pizza, she didn't like the school, she thought the house was small. Sam might have worried about this quite a lot, if Matthew hadn't rung the doorbell just then.

Matthew had freckles on his nose and a scar on his chin where he'd fallen off his bike. He had his skateboard under his arm.

'Do you want to come to the park?' he asked Sam. 'I'm going skateboarding.'

'My friend Cecily has arrived. I'll just ask her,' said Sam. She took Matthew into the lounge and introduced him to Cecily. 'Matthew says do we want to go skateboarding with him?'

'I've never been skateboarding,' said Cecily, but to Sam's relief she saw a glimmer of something familiar and reassuring in Cecily's eyes. There was a time when Cecily and Sam would have tried anything together, and they never ever said they were frightened, even if they were. Sam knew that Cecily had that feeling again, that tingly daring feeling of wanting to take a risk and try something new.

'Have you brought your jeans?' asked Sam. 'You can't go skateboarding dressed like that.'

When Cecily went upstairs to change, Matthew rolled his eyes. 'You didn't tell me your friend was so naff,' he said.

'Don't be mean. She's not naff,' said Sam, feeling she ought to defend Cecily. Then she added, 'At least, she never used to be naff.'

Cecily's jeans were new. They had that hard, uncomfortable look which jeans have until they've been washed about twenty times. Her trainers were new too. They had little silver stars on the sides, and pink laces.

On the way to the park, they had to walk past Joe Fenton and his friends who were hanging around outside the corner shop. Joe was fifteen and he always wore black leather clothes and studded wristbands, with a picture of a skeleton on his back. Everybody knew that Joe was a bit of a troublemaker, but when you lived near him you got used to him being around and learned how to deal with him. He saw Sam and Cecily and Matthew approaching, and stepped in front of them.

'Well, if it isn't little Samantha Coles,' he said in a high voice.

'Get out of my way, Joe Fenton,' said Sam.

'Who's your smart friend, Sam? It's not Cecily, is it? Hey guys, get this. Cecily's come back to see us. Slumming it, are you Cecily? I thought your mummy had decided you were too good for the likes of us.'

Matthew and Sam pushed past them and

continued up the hill to the park. Suddenly, Cecily burst into tears.

'It's so awful,' she sniffed. 'I was so frightened in case they did something terrible to us.'

'But you know Joe Fenton,' said Sam. 'He doesn't hurt people. He just thinks it's grown up to be rude.'

'I think he's a disgusting person,' said Cecily.

'His dad died when he was three, and he's got a really awful stepdad,' said Matthew. 'I think he's had a hard life. It's easy to be nice when you've got rich parents and a big house,' he added, and Sam knew he was getting at Cecily but she thought there wasn't much point, because Cecily didn't seem to realize he was talking about her.

Cecily took a lace hanky out of the pocket of her jeans and blew her nose.

Matthew sniffed. 'Yuk!' he said, 'Somebody's stepped in dog dirt.'

They all checked the bottom of their shoes. There, sticking to the bottom of Cecily's trainer and squashing up round the edge onto the silver stars, was a great big brown dollop.

Cecily burst into tears again. Sam found a stick and scraped her trainer and persuaded her to wipe it on the grass. She was beginning to think what fun Matthew and she would be having right now, if it weren't for Cecily.

In the park, Sam carried her skateboard to the top of the hill and whizzed down with her hair flying behind her. She could see that

Cecily was really impressed, but didn't want to show it.

'That's easy,' said Cecily. 'I can do that.'

'Go on then,' said Matthew, 'Try it.'

Sam thought Matthew was being a bit irresponsible. What if Cecily fell and hurt herself?

'Don't try it on this steep hill,' said Sam. 'Go over there where it's flatter and practise a few times first. I'll show you what to do.'

They practised all afternoon, and Cecily became more and more confident until at last she was laughing and shouting and behaving just like the Cecily Sam remembered. Sam thought perhaps they might still be the best friends in the world, even if Cecily did have a pony and frilly curtains.

Some children were throwing a ball for their dog nearby. Cecily was skateboarding down the hill, arms out at her sides, wobbling a bit, but managing to stay on. Then the red ball bounced across the path in front of her, and the dog leaped after it just as she was passing.

It yelped as the skateboard hit its leg. Cecily somersaulted off and landed on the path. She lay very still, and Sam had the most awful thoughts going through her mind as she ran down to help her. What if Cecily was dead, or really badly injured? It would all be her fault. She'd be responsible for killing her best friend in the whole world.

But by the time she got to her, Cecily had sat up and she was howling so loudly that

Sam thought she couldn't possibly be badly hurt. She'd torn the knees of her jeans and grazed her elbows and her forehead. Sam yelled at the children that they ought to be more careful about where they threw the ball, and they yelled back that her stupid friend ought to learn to skateboard properly instead of hurting their dog's leg.

Eventually, Sam and Matthew persuaded Cecily to hobble home between them. Sam's mother put plasters on Cecily's elbows and made her lie down on the settee.

'I want to go home,' whimpered Cecily. 'I don't like it here. I want my mummy.'

Sam could see that although her mum was sorry that Cecily had been hurt, she was also irritated. Sam didn't think that was very fair, because it wasn't Cecily's fault after all. The dog had run in front of her when she was still practising, and she didn't know how to stop. Sam or Matthew would have stopped in plenty of time, or they'd have done a wicked cool trick and whizzed round the dog instead of running into it. Maybe, when they were as good at skateboarding as Joe Fenton, they'd be able to ramp over the dog. She'd suggest to Matthew that they ought to spend lots of time in the park during the holidays, learning how to do really brill ramps.

Cecily's mother arrived an hour later.

'Oh, my poor baby,' she said when she saw Cecily. 'I think we'll have to have your head X-rayed. That's a nasty bump you've had.'

'I really don't think it needs an X-ray, Joan,' said Sam's mum.

'Some of us believe in taking care of our children, Julie,' said Cecily's mum. 'Quite frankly, I think it was very irresponsible to let them go off to the park by themselves like that. You've no idea what types might be hanging around there. And you've torn your nice new jeans, my sweetie pie,' she said to Cecily.

Sam thought Cecily's jeans looked much better with holes in the knees.

That night, her mum came into her bedroom and sat on her bed again. 'I'm sorry things didn't work out with Cecily,' she said.

Sam lay quietly, wondering if she ought to tell her mother what she was thinking. 'Mum, do you think the city's a dangerous place for children? Do you and dad ever think of taking us to live in the country?'

Her mother smiled. 'Life is full of dangers and challenges, Sam. I think we have to learn to meet the challenges rather than running away from them. I have a feeling that if Cecily had still been living next door, she'd have coped perfectly well with everything that happened today. Besides, we enjoy living in the city. I know it's dirty and littered and you get all sorts of odd people, but that's part of the attraction in a way. I don't think we're meant to live among people exactly like us all the time.' She laughed. 'Can you imagine living in a village where everybody is just like Joan?'

As Sam rolled over and switched off the

light, she wondered if Matthew would like to go to the cinema on the bus tomorrow. She didn't suppose Cecily ever went on buses now. Was there a cinema in the village, or did her mum have to drive her everywhere? She suddenly felt very sorry for Cecily, and decided she would keep writing to her, and she would still be her friend, because otherwise, she could not bear to think how lonely Cecily would be.

3

The dream
of an
African child

Kamuti lives in a village in Zimbabwe,
but she dreams of living in the city.
One night, she thinks her dream
has come true.

Kamuti lives in a village in Africa with her mother and father, her brothers and sisters, her grandparents, and all her aunts and uncles and cousins. There is much love in Kamuti's village, but not much money. The villagers keep chickens and goats, and they grow mealies on the land around the village. They keep some of their mealies to feed their own families, and they sell the rest to the Grain Marketing Board to be ground into mealie meal. They use the money to buy cooking oil, sugar, tea, and clothes for their children. The villagers always have enough of everything, but never too much of anything.

Kamuti has heard of places where people do not live in villages and grow crops, but they live in cities and work in offices. One day she looks up to see an aeroplane like a silver eagle high in the blue sky, and she thinks that when she grows up, she will fly on an aeroplane to another country and live in a city.

That night, she lies down on her mat beside her sister in their hut. The hut has a roof made of grass and walls made of mud. Inside it is warm with the breath of chickens and people. Kamuti closes her eyes and sleeps. The hut fades away as the stars fade when the first light of day appears in the sky. She can no longer hear the song of the frogs in the river. She can no longer hear the jackals wailing at the moon, or the breeze whispering to the leaves in the msasa trees.

Kamuti is in a city, a city as grey as the sky on a day in July, when thick clouds swallow the heat of the sun and people huddle close to the fire to keep warm. The buildings rise around her like the mountains where fisheagles fly and leopards prowl, but on these mountains there are no trees for hornbills to hide their young and monkeys to leap through the branches.

The pavement is hard beneath her bare feet. Nowhere can she see rich brown earth, as dark as a mother's skin, where chongololos crawl and snails make silvery trails, where pumpkin seeds lie hidden until the rains come to soak the ground. There are no rocks, round and smooth, for the lizard to warm his belly and the snake to shed his skin.

The city is a noisy place and a smelly place. Cars, lorries, buses and vans make the sound of a thousand bushfires.

Everywhere people are hurrying like the termites which build tall mounds near the village. The people are not smiling as Kamuti's father smiles when he sits outside the hut at the end of the day. Their faces are as worried as the baboon's when ticks burrow under his skin and make him itch.

There are shops which sell clothes and

food. Shops which sell books and pencils. Shops which sell radios and television sets and cars and toys. Kamuti has never seen so many shops. Children walk past eating food out of packets and drinking from cans. When they are finished, they throw down their rubbish as the jacaranda trees toss their purple blossoms to the ground when they have finished blooming.

Suddenly, Kamuti sees a person as familiar as the soft pink skin on her own palm coming towards her. It is her mother. But look! Her mother is trying to be like all the city women. She is wearing a red dress and her body smells like the poinsettia flower when you hold it too close to your nose, and its sweetness makes you sneeze.

Kamuti knows now how the newborn wildebeast feels when it loses its mother in the herd and runs calling and desperate on spindly legs. She longs for her grandmother's arms to close around her as wrinkled and warm as the skin on the eggplant after cooking.

'Mama,' she says, 'where are grandmother and grandfather?' Her mother laughs, but it is not the gentle laugh of the dove. It is the greedy laugh of the hyaena.

'They no longer live with us,' she says. 'We have sent them to an old people's home. People who live in the city are too busy to look after grandparents.'

'What are they busy doing?' asks Kamuti, wondering how people can be too busy when they do not have to hoe the fields or milk the goats or find where the hen has laid her eggs.

'They are busy making money to go shopping to buy food and clothes and motor cars,' says her mother.

'But mama, they already have too many clothes and too much food and their streets are full of motor cars. Why must they work to get more?'

'Ah my daughter,' says her mother, 'In our village, enough was always enough. But here in the city, too much is never enough.'

Kamuti looks around. All the people are too busy to notice her. Nobody smiles and says 'Hello Kamuti'. How can she live without her grandmother to comfort her when the dust devil blows or the red ant bites? How will she learn about the life of her people without her grandfather to tell her legends and stories of times long ago?

A motor bike passes with a roar louder than a hungry lion. The rider is dressed all in black, like the dark spirits which prowl in the night to frighten children. Kamuti is afraid. She runs into a building where machines clatter and whir, and people look at her as angrily as the buffalo when he prepares to charge.

Outside, it begins to rain. Dark clouds shut out the light and there is a howling noise like the wind which sweeps off the mountains. The machines explode and flash all around her. Kamuti screams.

Her sister rolls over and her body presses

warmly on Kamuti's arm. Her mother comes to her, as soft and comforting as sunshine after rain.

'Hush my daughter. You are dreaming. Perhaps you are afraid of the thunder and lightning. Outside it is raining, but inside our hut we are warm and dry.'

Kamuti buries her face against her mother's neck and smells the woodsmoke on her skin. She hears her grandmother snoring like a bushpig in the hut next door.

Now when Kamuti looks up at aeroplanes like silver eagles high in the African sky, she no longer dreams of going to a place where people have too much of everything, but not enough of anything.

4

The boy
with a toucan
in his heart

*The boy from the Amazon rainforest was
heartbroken when gold miners destroyed his
village and his way of life. Then he discovered
that some things can never be destroyed.*

The boy's people had always lived in the rainforest. They believed that at the beginning of time, their ancestors had climbed down to earth on a rope from heaven, and ever since then the forest had been theirs. They belonged in the forest as the fish belonged in the sea and the birds belonged in the air. It was theirs not to possess and destroy, but to nurture and enjoy. Generations of children had played under the green canopy, while their mothers gathered berries and nuts and their fathers hunted for food. The forest had been kind to the people who lived there, and they had come to share its secrets. They knew which plants were good to eat, and which plants had juices so poisonous that a drop on the tip of an arrow would kill the fiercest beast which crept through the undergrowth at night. The forest people celebrated just as nature herself celebrated, with feathers and flowers and colours and songs. They had great ceremonies, when the chief would wear his feathered headdress and mothers would paint their children's bodies with red and brown dyes squeezed from berries.

The forest people believed that the universe was round, and they built their villages in circles to reflect the never-ending roundness of creation. At night the boy would look up at the starry dome of the sky, and he would watch the smoke curling up from the fire, and he would hear the singing voices of his people, and he would think of a round universe, a perfect circle without a beginning or an end, a circle which was made up of the lives of all the generations that had ever been, and all the generations still to come.

But one day, the boy awoke to hear a new sound in the forest clearing. It was not the whisper of the morning breeze fanning leaves high above. It was not the surge of the river on its journey to the sea. It was not the gurgle of the frogs which lived along the river's edge, nor was it the chatter of the monkeys playing games in the treetops. This was a sound more sinister than the slither of the snake and more terrifying than the footfall of the jaguar. This was a sound which drowned out every other sound, a greater sound than the boy had ever heard before. It was as if a monster was snarling and crashing its way towards the village.

That day, the boy knew that the circle of life had been broken. He did not know where the beginning had been, but he knew that the end had come.

The lorries were yellow with tyres higher than the thatched roof on his house. Men with saws came in the lorries, and the saws had teeth like piranhas, teeth which chewed through the towering trees and sent them shuddering to the ground with a groan and a sigh and a trembling in their leaves. The men said they had come to dig a mine because there was gold buried in the ground. The boy thought that the trees were more beautiful and precious than gold. Did gold have branches where the black and orange toucan bird could build its nest? Did gold grow soft green leaves to shelter the people living in its shadow and protect the slow-moving sloth as it hung forever upside down among the trees? Did gold catch the sunbeams and make the shadows dance to the music of the wind? But there was no point in saying this to the men who came with saws, for who would listen to such a small boy?

The men built tin huts where the boy and his people lived for a while. Children played in the broken earth while their fathers searched endlessly for gold and their mothers worked with busy hands and frightened faces because there was so little food to give their children now that the forest had gone. Some of the men found gold and left the village. It was said that they went to a great city where they bought houses and motor cars, but the boy's father never found any gold. There was no money to pay for the food which once the forest had given freely to all who needed it. One day, the boy and his family packed their belongings and they too went to the city.

There were beautiful places in the city, where fountains sparkled in shady squares and shops spilled their fragrance into the air. People sat in cafes, eating and drinking and laughing with their friends. Cars were parked in gleaming rows along the pavement, and in suburbs nearby blue swimming pools glistened in gardens which were almost as green and fertile as the forest.

But the boy's family went to live in another part of the city where there were many others like them. This was not a place where people sang and danced and celebrated. This felt like a wilder place than the forest. Men fought in dusty streets and women cried. Children begged for food and babies wailed. The boy no longer lived in a protective circle of love, and he was afraid and lonely.

Then one night, as he lay on his mattress looking up at the corrugated roof and dreaming about the forest sky, he discovered a toucan hidden in his heart, in a place where nobody else could see it or feel it or hear it. It was a magnificent toucan, with glossy plumage and a curving orange bill. It was a toucan which would live with him forever, because it lived in a protective circle of love which nobody could ever take away or destroy.

The boy had discovered one of the great secrets of life. Inside every child there is a magic circle, a small universe where the things which children love live forever. After a while, he forgot the bare red earth and the river made muddy with dirt from the gold mine. He no longer remembered the fires they lit to burn

the forest so that the smoke lay like a blanket over the stars. He realized that these things cannot live for long, because nobody loves them enough to keep them alive.

He remembered the forest as it had been before the lorries came. He remembered the sunshine dancing greenly through the leaves and the faces of his people glowing golden in the firelight. He remembered the river reflecting the transparent sky, the silver ripple of fish and the clouds of butterflies which flew up from the grass around his ankles. He remembered the lap of the water against his canoe and the damp earth yielding beneath his feet.

He kept all these things alive with his love, and he heard the forest birds singing the song that his heart longed to sing. He dreamed of the day when the circle of life would be restored and the toucan would be set free and he would live in the forest forever, celebrating its goodness with all the generations that had ever been and all the generations still to come.

5

The shepherd boy

(based on a true story)

A shepherd in Peru was devastated by the death of his sheep. But then an angel appeared, wearing blue jeans and carrying a camera.

In years to come, Roberto would tell his friends that the angel who visited him that day really didn't look like an angel. He was wearing blue jeans and trainers, and instead of wings he had a camera slung round his neck. But he must have been an angel, for who else could have achieved such a miracle?

It had started as a day like any other. Roberto had woken up just as the dawn was licking the mountain ridges in the east. He had driven his family's sheep into the grassy slopes where they would graze for the day, while he sat underneath a tree and talked to his friends and dreamed of going to school, and wearing new clothes, and all the other impossible dreams which the children in his village had.

Of course they couldn't go to school. The nearest school was fifty miles away. And new clothes? Ha. They laughed and laughed at that, for what child in their village had ever owned new clothes? Their trousers and pullovers and skirts and hats were passed down from brother to brother and sister to sister, so that by the time they reached the youngest child, there were more patches than clothes.

The children sat on the sweet-smelling grass, and high overhead a condor soared on wide black wings to bring omens of good and evil to the people living in the mountains. Roberto leaned back on his elbows and watched the flight of the condor, while his sheep drifted like puffs of cotton towards the narrow dirt track which wound down the mountainside.

Roberto didn't hear the sound of an engine and the crunch of tires on the track. He didn't notice that his sheep had wandered onto the road. His friends were playing games, laughing and shouting in the crisp mountain air, so they weren't watching the sheep either.

There was a sudden crash and a terrible cry, and then a silence so deep and ominous that it was as if the sky had fallen to the ground. Roberto struggled to his feet and ran with his friends down to the track. The bodies of his sheep were strewn about the road, and the driver of the van was sitting with his head in his hands. Desperately, Roberto ran from one woolly body to the next, but all of his sheep were dead except for a lamb which had been born a few days earlier.

Roberto's family had no other wealth in the world. The sheep were their livelihood, their only security. Roberto gazed around at the faces of his friends and saw the horror in their brown eyes, then he turned and trudged up the slope to sit alone under a tree. Hot tears burned his cheeks and his shoulders shuddered in his blue pullover. How could he tell his parents this dreadful news? His family's future had been ruined, and all because he wasn't paying attention. He whispered a prayer to God, but he doubted if even God could put things right again.

After a while, he became aware of somebody standing beside him. Even though his eyes were closed, he sensed that somebody was standing between him and the sun, so that a shadow had fallen over him. He peeked between his fingertips to see a large pair of white trainers, newer and smarter than any he had seen before. Cautiously, he looked up. The man was wearing a T-shirt and he had a beard. The sun behind him made his blonde hair look a bit like a halo.

'Who are you?' asked Roberto tearfully.

'I'm a photographer. I've come here to take photographs of your beautiful country for my magazine. I saw what happened to your sheep. I'm so sorry.'

Roberto shrugged and lowered his eyes again. He didn't want to look down at the road, where the villagers had gathered and his mother was weeping over the dead sheep.

'Do you mind if I take your picture?' asked the man.

Roberto wanted to tell him to go away, but he knew that would be impolite. He wiped his eyes and tried to smile, but the tears just kept coming and his chin wouldn't stop wobbling,

so he didn't know what kind of picture the man would end up with.

The death of the sheep made life very hard for Roberto and his family. His parents still entrusted him with the lamb that had survived, and Roberto cherished the little creature as if his life depended on it, which in a way it did. He kept his eyes on the lamb from the moment he took it up to the pastures in the morning, to the moment he returned to the village in the evening, and he never lifted his eyes to look up at the blue sky and the distant mountain peaks. If he had, he might have noticed an aeroplane like a silver condor catching the sparkle of sunlight high overhead, bringing with it the best news that had ever been heard in the village.

The photographer had printed his photographs of Roberto's country, and people had marvelled at the wild beauty of the mountains and the green tranquillity of the valleys. But they had also seen the picture of the grief-stricken shepherd boy and they had read about the fate of his sheep. Many readers had sent money to the photographer, asking him to find the boy and replace the sheep which had been killed. So the photographer had come again on an aeroplane to Roberto's country, and he had set out in search of the village high in the mountains where Roberto lived.

There was enough money to replace all the sheep, with enough left over to build a school in the village for the children who lived there.

Roberto picked up the lamb he had been caring for, and this time he smiled for the photographer.

'God will repay you,' he said, and he laughed to think that angels came in such strange disguises.

6
Rosita's miracle

Miracles don't happen ... or do they?
A Spanish girl experienced a kind of
miracle when her parents met at the foot
of a weeping statue.

'Que miraglo!' What a miracle! Tongues were clacking like castanets in the small Spanish town. Rosita's mother pretended not to be interested.

'Huh,' she said, tossing her head. 'They say that the Madonna is crying in *l'Eglesia de Nuestra Señora de la Mercede*. I ask you, did you ever hear of anything so ridiculous? A stone statue, crying. They say the tears are running down her face. Hundreds of people have gone to see. They must be crazy!'

She sat down at the kitchen table opposite Rosita, and her dark eyes burned in the gloom.

'Your father and I were married in that church,' she said. 'I was twenty-two and he was twenty-four. He was so handsome Rosita, ah, I wish you could have seen him. And I was beautiful. I did not have these grey hairs then.'

Rosita stared at her mother across the table. Outside in the courtyard, the vivid colours of the geraniums were fading into night. She couldn't see her mother's grey hairs in that light. She could only see her olive skin and gleaming black eyes. It was easy to imagine her as a young and beautiful bride, when the sunlight did not show the bitter lines around her mouth and the anger in her eyes, which made her look more severe than she really was.

Rosita's parents no longer lived together. She could remember a time, long ago when she was very young, when they laughed together and there was the murmur of happy voices when she lay in bed at night. But then the voices became angry and the laughter disappeared, and one day her father packed his belongings and went to live in another part of town.

Her mother frowned and her face darkened, the way it did when she thought of the man she had married. 'I gave him everything,' she said. 'I should not have married such a scoundrel. He was useless, Rosita, he was a bad man, believe me. If I ever see him again, I shall spit in his face. You can be sure of that.'

Rosita knew there was no point in arguing, although her father was not a bad man. He had laughing eyes and a gentle smile, and when he took her out he did everything he could to make her happy. He said he was sorry that things had become so bad between her mother and himself.

'Come Rosita,' said her mother, standing up and snapping her fingers. 'Eat your dinner. Hurry up or we shall be late.'

'Where are we going?' Rosita asked.

'We're going to see the crying Madonna, of course,' said her mother.

They walked along the narrow winding roads to the Plaza. Women leaned over wrought iron balconies, calling to one another.

'Have you heard about the miracle?'

Rosita's mother laughed. 'Pah! What miracle! This is a childish story!' But there was an excited spring in her step, and she walked so quickly that Rosita had to run and skip to keep up with her. 'Miracles,' she kept muttering as she went. 'There is no such thing as a miracle.'

Rosita was breathless and panting by the time they reached the Plaza and pushed their way through the chattering huddles of people into the cool church with its glowing candles and smell of incense in the air.

A crowd had gathered around the feet of the statue. Some were fingering rosaries and praying, others were crying. It was a miracle, they all said, a miracle.

'See the tears flowing down her face, falling onto the ground at her feet.'

Rosita stared at the statue, but it was too dark to see whether she was crying or not.

'She is smiling, look, she is smiling,' said one woman.

'And see how she is swaying,' said another. 'She is swaying backwards and forwards. Que miraglo!'

But Rosita was no longer paying attention.

Standing near them in the crowd was her father. She wondered what would happen if her mother saw him. Would she really spit in his face, there, in front of all those people? Rosita glanced up at the Virgin and prayed that her parents would not see each other.

She watched and waited, while all around her the people murmured and exclaimed and marvelled. She saw her father looking around, then he noticed her and his eyes lit up in recognition and his face crinkled in a loving smile. He looked beyond Rosita, and saw his wife standing beside her. He came closer, moving quickly through the crowd so that by the time her mother saw him it was too late to move away.

'Teresa,' he said. Rosita saw the shock on her mother's face, then the strange, uncertain smile.

'Hello Enrique,' she said.

'Have you come to see the miracle?' her father asked.

'There is no such thing,' said her mother.

They looked at each other, as if not knowing what to say next. They seemed young and nervous. Rosita had never seen them that way before.

'Do you remember this church, Teresa?' her father asked.

'Of course,' said her mother, trying to sound disinterested.

'You were a fine bride, Teresa,' her father said.

Her mother paused, glanced up at him, and then said, 'I was marrying a fine man, Enrique.'

'Que miraglo!' declared the crowd. A woman rushed in from outside.

'The moon has risen over the rooftops and it is dancing in the sky,' she said.

'The stars are also dancing,' said another.

'There is a wonderful smell of roses in the air,' cried another.

Rosita's mother looked up at Enrique and he looked down at her.

'I miss you, Teresa,' he said.

She lowered her eyes. Did she sway a little? Were there tears on her cheeks? Rosita wasn't sure. Perhaps it was just the candlelight playing tricks on her senses.

Her father reached out and took her mother's hand. 'Have you and Rosita eaten?' he asked. 'Can I take you both out for supper?'

'I cooked her favourite meal,' said her mother, 'but she left half of it on her plate. I'm sure she's still hungry.'

Rosita followed her parents out of the church and into the darkening Plaza. The red tiled roofs glowed warmly in the moonlight. Silver moonbeams rested on the heads of the people gathered there, talking of miracles. Rosita's feet tripped lightly over the uneven cobbles. She saw her mother slip her arm through her father's, and she smiled and murmured to herself, 'Que miraglo!'

Much later, as they sat under the stars at a small table with a checked cloth, Rosita fell asleep with her head on her father's shoulder while her parents talked about the years they had spent together. Then she felt his strong arms lifting her up and carrying her home, and tucking her in to her small wooden bed.

She woke up the next morning and remembered the miracle. She ran through to her parents' bedroom.

'Where is papa?' she asked.

'He has gone home of course,' said her mother.

'But it was a miracle. You are going to stay together, aren't you?'

Her mother laughed, and her laughter was as soft as the sunshine which trickled through the window onto her face.

'No, my Rosita, we can't stay together. He has his life now, and I have mine. We both realized that last night. Hush my daughter, why are you crying? Come. Come here.'

Rosita sat on the bed beside her mother, and her mother stroked her hair. There was a new gentleness in her touch, and the severe lines around her mouth had gone.

'To think that if we hadn't gone to the church last night, we wouldn't have met. There are so many things we wouldn't have talked about. It was good to laugh with him again Rosita, to discover that we are still friends. Perhaps it is a miracle of sorts, eh Rosita? Just a small miracle maybe, but a miracle all the same. Come now, dry your eyes and get dressed. Your father is taking you out for the day, and afterwards he'll have supper with us before he goes home.'

Rosita looked at her mother, sitting against white pillows with her face gilded by sunlight. She sighed, but deep inside her a small voice whispered, 'Que miraglo', as she went to her room to get ready for her father.

7

Tsitsi's Christmas

Tsitsi lived in a poor township in Africa. Alone in the house one Christmas Eve, she experienced for herself the meaning and the mystery of Christmas.

It was Christmas Eve. Tsitsi sat on the kitchen floor next to the stove. Her mother had gone to work and Tsitsi was comforted by the warmth of the stove and the clutter of the cooking pots.

Tsitsi knew that her mother had to work, but she couldn't help wishing that they were together on this special night when other families were celebrating. Her mother had explained that many people came into town on Christmas Eve, and she could earn enough to buy a chicken for Christmas lunch, and perhaps even a present for Tsitsi. But as Tsitsi sat in the kitchen, she thought she would rather be with her mother than have chicken and a present.

When Tsitsi's mother went to work in the bars in the city, she wore a shiny red dress and black high-heeled shoes. She wore make up too, and perfume. The perfume lingered in the air long after she had gone, but although it reminded her of her mother, Tsitsi did not like the smell. When her mother was dressed up like that, she was like a stranger.

Tsitsi felt close to her mother on nights when she did not go out to work, when she put on her old yellow dressing gown and they sat together in the kitchen, drinking tea and talking to each other. Sometimes she would take Tsitsi on her knee.

'One day I will marry a good man, Tsitsi,' she would say. 'Then I'll be able to stay home with you every night. I'll never have to leave you alone.'

Tsitsi counted those evenings among her beautiful moments, memories which glistened like stars against the darkness of everyday life and comforted her at times when she was cold and hungry and lonely. Sometimes she invented beautiful moments which had not really happened but which made her happy just to think about. Occasionally, she felt she was close to understanding something very important. It was as if there was something more wonderful than anything she could dream of, beyond the scope of her imagination. Even her most beautiful thoughts could not capture this other beauty, but she always sensed it was there, and she believed that one day she would know what it was.

But it was especially difficult that Christmas Eve, for not only was she alone, but outside there was a thunderstorm. Rain pounded on the tin roof of her house, lightning streaked through the torn curtain, and thunder rattled all the window panes.

There was the pain too. It was not new, this pain in her head, but lately it had been getting worse. She had told her mother about it, and her mother had said that she would take her to the clinic after Christmas. Tonight her mother had given her aspirin before she went out, but still the pain was there, and it distracted Tsitsi from her dreams. She closed her eyes and rested her head in her hands, and imagined a Christmas full of beautiful moments.

She thought of a warm room, with pictures on the walls and thick curtains to keep out the lightning. In a corner of the room there was a Christmas tree glittering with lights. Under the tree was a pile of parcels, tied with bright ribbons and bows, waiting for children to open them. Tsitsi knew that these things were part of Christmas, because she had seen them in shop windows when her mother took her to town.

In the centre of the room was a table laden with her favourite food, and around the table were Tsitsi's brothers and sisters, her grandparents, all the people who made up the loving family of her dreams. Her mother was smiling and laughing, and her father was there too.

Tsitsi had never known her father, but she had in her mind a picture of the man she would like to call father. This man was not like any of the men her mother brought to the house. Some of these spoke kindly to her, but most of them ignored her. A few had even pushed her and spoken rudely to her, but she preferred to forget about them.

Her father at the table was no one she had ever met before. But she would know him at once if she ever did meet him.

Her head was hurting terribly. She bit her lip and tried not to cry out.

Then her eyes widened and her heart began to pound in fear. Over the noise of the storm, she could hear someone knocking at the door.

Tsitsi had heard of the thieves who prowled in the township at night. Her mother had warned her never to open the door when she was alone, so she covered her ears with her hands and tried to ignore the sound. But the knocking continued, and she thought she could hear a voice. It was a man's voice.

'Help us, please, we need your help.'

Tsitsi knew that she should not open the door. It might be somebody trying to trick her, somebody who knew that she was alone. But what if it was someone in need, standing outside in the rain? Someone who might be in pain, like herself. Someone who was also lonely, or afraid of the storm. She stood up and walked slowly to the door. She tried to look through the keyhole but she could see nothing.

'What do you want?' she called in a small voice.

'Please help us. My wife needs shelter,' shouted the man above the clatter of the rain. 'She is about to have her baby. We were going to the hospital, but the rain has delayed us and the baby is coming now.'

Tsitsi pulled back the bolt and opened the door. The man on the doorstep was holding a bicycle, and on the saddle sat a young woman with wide, anxious eyes. Her clothes were wet and she was shivering.

'Please come in,' said Tsitsi.

The woman looked frightened, and Tsitsi spoke very gently to reassure her.

'Come,' she said, 'You must take off those wet clothes.'

She gave the woman her mother's dressing gown and helped her into the bed which she shared with her mother in a corner of the kitchen. She made tea and gave the man some of the bread which they had been saving for Christmas lunch.

Then she watched as the woman gave birth to a baby son.

She stood beside the bed and saw the woman's face relax as she held her newborn child. Tsitsi thought she had never seen anyone who looked so loving.

But even the joy of the baby's birth did not ease the pain in her head, which was blurring her eyesight and making her feel dizzy and ill.

'What's the matter?' asked the woman. 'Aren't you feeling well?'

Tsitsi nodded, unable to speak.

'Come,' said the woman, 'lie here beside me,' and she moved across to make space for Tsitsi.

Gratefully, Tsitsi climbed onto the bed and snuggled down beside the familiar feel of her mother's dressing gown.

'Would you like to hold the baby?' asked the woman.

'Oh yes please,' breathed Tsitsi, and the woman placed the tiny body in her arms. Tsitsi held the baby close and felt his warmth against her, and then the most wonderful thing happened.

The pain in her head disappeared.

She gazed down at the small brown face and dark eyes, and we will never know exactly what happened next. Perhaps she fell asleep and began to dream, or maybe it was just another of her fantasies. Or was it something else?

As she looked at him, he seemed to change. He was no longer a baby lying in her arms. He was a man, standing beside the bed and smiling down at her. He was the person she knew so well, the person she had been waiting for all her life.

'Father!' she said.

He held his arms out to her.

'I've come to take you home, Tsitsi,' he said. 'I've prepared a room for you. A room with a Christmas tree and a wonderful feast on the table. Your family is there waiting for you.'

When he smiled, she knew that this was the beautiful moment she had been waiting for. This was the source of all the other beautiful moments she had ever known. She had found it at last.

She smiled back at him and slipped her hand into his.

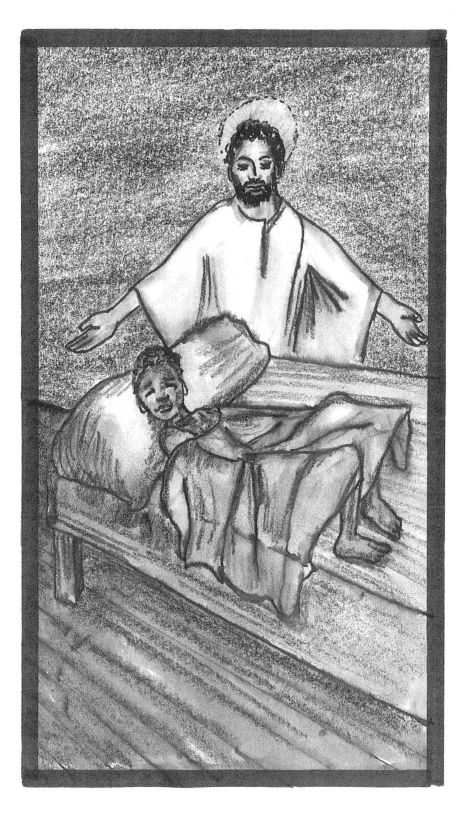

Her mother found her the next morning, curled up in bed beside the yellow dressing gown. She was smiling, because at last Tsitsi was enjoying a beautiful moment which would last forever.

8

The
desert sky

*This is the story of Suad, an Arab child
caught up in the Gulf War, dreaming of peace
and of a seemingly forgotten
angels song.*

Suad sat on the end of her bed, looking out of the window. Often before she had stared into the blue black sparkle of night, and she had been glad of the walls around her pushing back the darkness. The desert was cold at night, but her house was warm. The sky and the desert were too vast for a child to understand, but her house was as secure as her mother's arms.

But houses were no longer secure, and the sky had become a hiding place for many terrors. Aeroplanes sliced through the night, showering bombs on the villages below so that walls crumbled and the darkness came rushing in.

Suad did not understand the reasons for the war. Her mother said it was madness, but her father and her uncles had gone to fight like all the other men in the village. Even her fourteen-year-old brother had gone. Only the women and children were left, and the white-haired men with stooping backs who were too old to fight.

Now her mother sat in the kitchen with her friends, and she stroked the mound of her belly in her long black robe, and with a lonely crooning in her voice she begged God to pro-

tect her unborn child. 'I pray that it is a girl. If it is a son, then let him never go to war. When he is fifteen, twenty, forty, will he want to go to fight against other women's sons? What is the point in that, I ask you, what is the point? War is madness. It betrays the women who struggle to give birth, who go hungry so that their children can eat.'

Suad looked out of the window and she dreamed of stopping the war. She leaned her chin on her hands on the windowsill and she imagined a world where the night was innocent as it used to be long ago, serene and silent, soothing people to sleep.

She drifted away from her small room with its square of light oozing from the window, away from the narrow streets and crooked doorways of the village, up and up, until she was floating high above the world she knew and her village was a cluster of buildings in the moonlit desert.

This, she thought, was what the village looked like to the men who flew over in aeroplanes late at night. Perhaps they didn't know that children were asleep down there. They couldn't see the women sitting in the kitchen, afraid of the howl of the jets. Maybe they thought their bombs fell on empty houses. She was sure that if the pilots knew there were people living there, they would not release their bombs.

Suad floated so high into the air that she felt she could reach out and touch the shadows on the moon. She felt free up there, and safe. Higher than bombs. Higher than her mother's fear which filled the house, even when she smiled and pretended not to be afraid. Higher than the houses with their fragile walls.

The sky around her rippled into life, the way froth rippled on the sea when it reached the shore. The night was white with angel wings, and the angels were singing a song as gentle as the morning breeze among the palm trees.

Long ago we sang to earth,
a glad song
long ago.

Peace on earth,
peace and goodwill.

Shepherds heard and wise men too
our angel voices
bright
setting the stars alight
above the ocean waters
catching heaven's glow
to toss it back
to angel hands.

One star broke free,
flared out and travelled
silently
across the desert sky.
Wide it travelled, high,

guided by a hidden hand
above the sleeping world,
to rest
above a stable,
lonely, cold,
gilding the dreams
of a mother
and her child.

Long ago.

The angel voices faded away and their wings
dissolved in the moonlight. Then the sky was
stirring, ruffling, angel voices sighing like the
dry sirocco wind which swirled around the
dunes while wings like storm clouds scudded
across the stars.

Tonight we sang to earth
again
but no one cared,
no one heard
the angel song.

Shepherds, wise men, all are gone,
tonight it's soldiers who keep watch,
so young, so young.

The light is drowned
in oil
and seabirds limp on broken wings
like angels
dying.

One star
brighter than the rest
flares out and whines
across the desert sky
to travel high
and guided by
what hidden hands?
It finds
the stable once again
and steals
the dreams
of mothers
and their children.

Suad closed her eyes and listened. Angelic voices mingling, hope and sorrow, light and dark, the sky alive with music. Surely, surely the world could hear. Then close, too close, a jet plane rushed out of the darkness, the roar of its engines drowning the voices and sending feathers fluttering to the far corners of the night.

She opened her eyes. She was sitting on her small bed, and far, far above her was the blue black sparkle of the night. The roar was fading away, and the last blink of the aeroplane's lights disappeared among the stars.

The stars were clean and white, beautiful because the sky was so dark.

She thought of her father coming home. She would run to him, and he would lift her up in his arms, and for a moment there would be no war. One day soon the baby would be born, and she would hold her newborn brother or sister, and for a moment there would be no war. In a little while her mother would come in to kiss her goodnight, and she would close her eyes and hold up her face, and for a moment there would be no war. Moments like stars in the dark, dark night.

Why did the stars shine only in darkness?

Suad lay down and closed her eyes, and angel voices rose like stars above the dark lament. Peace on earth, goodwill to all the people. She longed for the day when peace would dazzle like the sun, chasing away the cold glimmer of starlight.

9

The brothers

When Pandit and Suresh were growing up in an Indian village, they dreamed of becoming rich and famous. As adults, they found fulfilment in unexpected ways.

Pandit and Suresh grew up in a village on the banks of the wide River Ganges. They remembered their childhood with the warm, happy feelings which people have when they live in an adult world and look back on the days of their youth. The smell of the frangipani blossoms on the evening breeze reminded them of the small garden outside their parents' home. The sight of water buffalo glimpsed from a fast-moving train brought memories of flooded paddy fields. The sizzle of spices frying in ghee reminded them of their grandmother's kitchen, of curries which brought a shimmer of sweat to their skin and chapatis which she patted and shaped in floury hands.

Like children everywhere, the boys had dreamed of what they would be when they grew up. When they were very young, their dreams were extravagant.

'I will be a prince,' said Pandit. 'I will marry a beautiful princess. I will wear a silk turban on my head and velvet slippers on my feet. I will live in a palace with a courtyard and magnificent banqueting rooms.'

'I'm going to be a film-star,' said Suresh. 'I'll go to Hollywood and I'll buy an expensive car and dark sunglasses. I will have hundreds of girlfriends.'

As the boys grew older, their dreams became more reasonable.

'Perhaps I'll be a doctor,' said Pandit. 'I'll go to medical school and open a clinic in an expensive suburb in the city. Rich people will pay me to cure them. I will wear smart clothes and everybody will respect me.'

'I might become a scholar,' said Suresh. 'I will work in a university where clever people will come to learn from me and I will write articles and books which will make me famous.'

When the boys were teenagers, their mother took them to the teeming city of Calcutta. Pandit and Suresh had never imagined there were so many people in the whole world, let alone in one city. Not only that, but they had not realized how many poor people there were. Blind men and pregnant women huddled in doorways with their arms outstretched. Children in rags asked for money. Old people hobbled past on twisted limbs and begged for food.

'I always thought our family was poor,' Suresh said to his mother, 'but I've never seen people as poor as this.'

'Our family is not poor,' said his mother. 'It's true, we never had money for luxuries, for fine clothes and expensive food, but we live well, my children. That's why I have brought you here. You are young. I hope you'll remember what you have seen today when you decide what to do with your lives.'

The boys weren't sure what she meant but she refused to explain.

Some weeks later, they were sitting together underneath the banyan tree in the cool of evening.

'I've been thinking of what our mother told us,' said Pandit. 'I have decided that I will spend my life helping those poor people we saw in the city.'

'Yes, I have been thinking the same thing,' said Suresh.

Pandit fulfilled his childhood dream by going to medical school and becoming a doctor, but he did not open a clinic in an expensive suburb. Instead, he went to work in a hospital in one of the poorest parts of the city, and for many years he worked among the poor, healing the sick and comforting the dying. He came to be known and loved throughout the narrow, crowded streets. Wherever he went, people called his name and raised their hands in greeting. Pandit worked tirelessly, going without sleep for many days and nights. People marvelled at his strength and his patience. It was a miracle, they said, that he could work with so little rest.

After many years, Pandit decided to return to his childhood village to see his family. His mother's face was wrinkled and her hair was white, but she ran to greet him with a happy laugh.

Suresh also came to greet Pandit. Suresh had become a holy man. He wore a long yellow robe and his face was smooth and serene. Pandit hid his resentment when he saw his brother, but later, when they were sitting again underneath the old banyan tree, Pandit voiced his feelings.

'Do you remember all those years ago, my brother, when we said that we would spend our lives helping the poor?'

'I remember,' smiled Suresh, gazing at the distant river where the last light of day was dancing on the water.

'I've kept my promise,' said Pandit. 'For all these years, I've been living and working among the poor, but you've been living in the temple, reading holy books and praying. You have done nothing for the poor.'

Suresh turned to his brother and the setting sun cast a warm glow on his skin.

'Pandit, I have heard talk of you. People have come to the temple and spoken of the doctor in the city who never grows tired, who works with miraculous strength, who shows love and compassion to all his patients, who is never too busy to spend time with the people who come to see him. Is this true?'

'It's true that I don't grow tired. Sometimes, when I think surely this work will defeat me, it's as if a fire begins to burn inside me, giving me new energy and hope. The more I do, the more I am able to do. The more love I show to people, the more love I find within myself.'

Suresh nodded and Pandit saw great wisdom in his eyes.

'I've prayed for you, Pandit, every day and every night in my temple. I know that you are too busy to pray, too busy to be quiet, so I have prayed for you to be given strength, I have been quiet for you so that in my silence you might find rest. Together, we have fulfilled our promise.'

Pandit felt so ashamed he couldn't lift his eyes to look at Suresh.

'I've judged you wrongly, my brother. In my work, there are people who know what I'm doing and who praise me for it. I am given gratitude and love by those around me. But you are alone. Even I haven't been grateful for your help, because I have not been aware of it.'

'My prayers would be of no use without your work,' said Suresh.

'But I wonder if I could do my work without your prayers,' said Pandit.

The brothers walked back to their mother's house and they saw her waiting for them in the doorway. They smiled and waved to her as she came to meet them.

'I am so proud of my sons,' she said. 'You have both fulfilled all the hopes I had for you.'

10

The china lady

Lucy was handicapped and confined to a
wheelchair. She dreamed of being as beautiful
as the china lady on her mother's shelf, until
she discovered the true nature of beauty.

There was one ornament in Lucy's house which was more beautiful than any other. It was a china lady which stood on the dresser in the lounge. The lady was wearing a long blue dress with a full skirt, and she had a parasol over her shoulder. The china was so delicate that her parasol looked like lace, and there was a soft pink blush to her skin. Once, Lucy's mother had taken the lady down and held her against Lucy's cheek. Lucy had felt how cool and smooth she was, how perfect in every way, and she had imagined being like the china lady, tying her hair with ribbons and carrying her parasol in a dainty hand in a white glove. She thought of petticoats rustling about her ankles, and soft leather shoes with pointed toes and high heels. She would walk lightly through town, nodding and smiling at passers-by, and the breeze would tug the ribbons in her hair and ruffle her dress as she went. People would stop and stare at her, and say how beautiful she was.

People did stare at Lucy when she went to town, not because she was beautiful but because she was different. Lucy couldn't walk at all, and when her mother pushed her wheelchair in crowded places, people would shake their heads and click their tongues and say, 'Isn't it a shame.' Lucy would ask them, 'Isn't what a shame?' but that only made them worse. Sometimes she was surprised that their heads didn't fall off altogether and go bouncing off down the street like lots of rubber balls with curly hair and sunglasses. Lucy couldn't walk, but she couldn't talk either, so when she said 'Isn't what a shame?' it sounded like 'shannit wawa shum?', so that only Lucy knew what she was saying, and sometimes her mother because her mother had spent years listening very carefully and trying to understand what Lucy meant when she spoke.

Even when people smiled at Lucy, she really thought they looked quite miserable – more miserable in fact than when they weren't smiling. Lucy knew what real smiles looked like, crinkly smiles which went all the way up to people's eyes. But when people looked at Lucy with smiling mouths and sad eyes and said, 'Poor little thing,' she just couldn't help laughing because they looked so funny, like sad clowns in a circus. Poor things, she would say to herself, wishing they enjoyed life as much as she did.

When Lucy smiled, her whole body seemed to smile. Her legs flew out and her arms flapped and her head danced and her eyes sparkled and everybody knew that Lucy was pleased about something. But not many people showed their pleasure as enthusiastically as Lucy did.

One day when they were shopping, a woman

said to her mother, 'Isn't it tragic? Was she born that way?' Lucy looked at the woman's hair and she thought that was a bit tragic too – had the woman been born with purple hair, or had she had an accident with a paintpot? She said, 'Am sashy purrup aye,' which meant, 'I'm sorry about your purple hair,' but the woman tutted away up the street, shaking her head and saying, 'Terrible, you'd think they'd put her away somewhere.' Lucy's mother muttered, 'Silly old cow,' under her breath, and then she said, 'Come on Lucy, let's treat ourselves to an icecream in that cafe over there.'

Lucy loved going to cafes, even though eating icecream was something of a problem for her as more of it tended to go in her ears and up her nose than in her mouth.

There was a man at another table in the cafe who kept staring at her, and she couldn't help staring back because he had such a strange face. His mouth was turned down at the corners and his nostrils were flared so that he looked rather like a pig. Lucy was so busy staring at him that she missed again and jammed her icecream on the end of her nose. The man shook his head and left without eating his chocolate cake or finishing his coffee. On the way past he said to Lucy's mother, 'It's disgusting, bringing someone like that into a public eating place.' Tears welled up in the eyes of Lucy's mother, and there might have been quite a scene, but, perhaps by accident, just at that moment Lucy's arm jerked out the

way it did sometimes, and the rest of her
icecream stuck to the back of his jacket and
slithered all the way down his trousers without him knowing. Lucy and her mother
laughed, and some people at the next table
saw what had happened and they laughed too,
and passers-by stopped and laughed, and soon
everybody in the whole street was laughing
except the man, who didn't know what they
were laughing about.

One day, Lucy's parents gave her some
modelling clay. The physiotherapist had said
it would be good for her to play with clay, so
they put a lump of it on her wheelchair tray
and pushed her into the lounge and left her
there to play. She stared up at the china lady,
then she looked down at the bright pink clay
on her tray, and she had an idea. Her mother
loved ornaments. She collected china animals,
china people, china plates, china vases – anything that was delicate and beautiful. Lucy
decided that she would make her mother an
ornament.

All afternoon she worked on the clay. Every
time her mother or father came in to check on
her, she laughed and shouted so that they
would know she was enjoying herself and
wanted to be left alone. But really, she wasn't
enjoying herself very much. In fact, she was
getting more and more discouraged.

Lucy knew exactly what she wanted to
make. She wanted to make a china man who
would stand next to the china lady. He would

be tall and handsome, with sleek hair and a black tailcoat and a white shirt and patent shoes with buttons on them. He would be a man who was worthy of the china lady's love.

But all she had was a lump of pink clay, and hands which wouldn't do what she wanted them to do, no matter how hard she tried. When she tried to squeeze the clay to make his legs, her hand jerked and poked a hole through his middle. When she tried to make his arms, her hands squeezed together so that he came oozing out between her fingers. Then, after hours of squeezing and jerking and pushing, she dropped him. He rolled off her wheelchair onto the floor, and there he lay, out of reach, a blob of pink clay with dents in all the wrong places and a hole in his middle.

Her mother came in and saw the clay on the floor. Lucy tried hard not to cry. Her mother bent down and picked the clay up very gently, cradling it in her hands. 'Did you make this?' she asked. Lucy grunted. 'Oh Lucy, Lucy it's wonderful.' Her voice sounded strange – thick and trembly, as if she might be about to cry. She called Lucy's father, and together they stood looking at the clay and then at Lucy. Lucy looked at the clay too. It looked like a mess to her, but they must see something which she couldn't. They really did seem to like it. She tried to tell them it was a present for them and her mother watched her face very closely, the way she did when she was trying to understand what she was saying.

Then she kissed Lucy and said, 'It's a lovely present. I shall keep it forever.' To Lucy's astonishment, she cleared a space beside the china lady and put the pink blob of clay there, so that it might have been a man after all, if you used your imagination. A handsome man who was in love with the china lady.

The clay stayed up there until it was dry and hard, and whenever visitors came to the house, Lucy's mother would show them the ornament that Lucy had made. It was there for so long that it began to look as if it belonged there, among all the beautiful and delicate ornaments.

Then one day, when Lucy was alone in the room, Petrocelli the cat leaped up on the dresser. Petrocelli was a huge black tom cat, much too big to be on such a narrow shelf with so many precious ornaments. Lucy tried to shout a warning to her mother, but her mother was busy and she wasn't concentrating, so she didn't understand what Lucy was saying. A fly buzzed past Petrocelli's nose, and he leaped up to catch it. Lucy watched in horror as his tail flicked against the ornaments, and first the china lady, then her pink man, were knocked to the floor and smashed.

Her mother heard the crash and came in. 'Oh no,' she said. 'What's happened?' Lucy groaned to tell her mother how sorry she was that the lady was broken. Her mother stared at the mess on the floor and she burst into

tears. Lucy cried too. She couldn't bear to see her mother so sad. She knew that the lady had been her favourite ornament. She wished she wasn't stuck in a wheelchair. If only she were free, she would go to the shops and buy her mother another one to replace her. Her mother gathered up the bits of the lady and threw them in the bin. Then she knelt down and carefully picked up the pieces of Lucy's man and put them on the dresser. 'Maybe daddy will be able to stick it together,' she said. 'Oh Lucy, it was the most precious thing I've ever been given. I can't believe it's broken.' Lucy realized that her mother wasn't crying for the china lady after all. She had hardly noticed as she threw the smooth white bits of china in the bin. It was the pink man she was crying for, the funny lumpy piece of clay which Lucy had made.

Later, Lucy watched in amazement as her father stuck the clay together and put it back on the shelf. She was amazed because he did it with such care and such love, and all the while her mother watched and told him exactly where each piece should go, and what it should look like.

After that, when Lucy sat in her wheelchair and looked at her pink man, she felt the funniest feeling inside. It was not the kind of happiness which made her squeal and flap her arms and nod her head and laugh. It was a quiet, warm feeling, the kind of feeling she sometimes had when her parents carried her up to bed, and wrapped their arms around her, and told her how much they loved her.

Lucy had discovered that it wasn't being perfect which made something precious and beautiful. It was being loved. She thought that must have made her one of the most beautiful children in the world.

11

The caterpillar tree

Life on the caterpillar tree was peaceful and happy until Bartholomew arrived. Could Bert, the humble brown caterpillar, restore it to its former happiness?

Long ago in the beginning of time there was a tree. It was probably the most beautiful tree there has ever been. It's bark was glossy and it's branches were covered in leaves and laden with apples. The tree was inhabited by a colony of caterpillars, and they lived there in perfect happiness. There was nothing to quarrel about and nothing to worry about. From morning to night they wriggled around the tree with such a variety of movements that they recognised each other by the way they moved. There was Sebastian Squirm and Wilma Wiggle, Suzie Scurry and Lionel Loop-a-Lot, Harry Hurry and Sybil Slow. Sybil was the oldest caterpillar on the tree, and Lionel was the fattest. Wilma was very long and thin, and Suzie was small, being the youngest. Everybody loved Suzie. Some of the caterpillars were green and some were brown. Some were hairy and some were smooth. They enjoyed the fact that they were all different. They thought it made life on the tree more interesting.

Then one day a stranger arrived on the tree, and he was so exceptionally different that they all stared and stared. His name was Bartholomew and he had an enormous green body with yellow stickers on his feet and blue spots on his back. The caterpillars had never seen such a magnificent creature. He moved very slowly, squelching and squidging along the branches with his rolls of fat rippling as he went. When he reached the glossiest, juiciest apple on the tree, he stopped and looked round at all the other caterpillars. They never criticised or grumbled about each other, but when he started to speak they had to admit, he had a most unpleasant voice.

'I claim this apple for my home,' he said, grinning. 'From now on, this is Bartholomew's property.' With that, he stuck a sign in the apple which said, 'Keep Out! Trespassers will be prosecuted!'

'You've made a mistake, Bartholomew,' said Suzie. 'Nobody needs to claim property on the tree. We share everything, and the fruit has never run out since time began.'

Now, it must be said here that if Suzie had known Bartholomew, she wouldn't have dared to speak to him like that. NOBODY accused Bartholomew of making mistakes. But in those days, the caterpillars did not understand the meaning of fear. Nothing had ever happened to threaten them or frighten them. So when Suzie looked up at Bartholomew's great body and leering mouth, she didn't feel the least bit afraid. But Bartholomew glared down at her with such a peculiar yellow glint in his eyes, and such a mean look about his mouth, that she felt a little tremor under her skin and all her legs began to shake.

'Come here, you impertinent invertebrate,' he said.

Suzie looked around. She didn't know anybody with that name.

'It's you I'm talking to,' he said.

'Who me?' said Suzie. By now, her legs were shaking so much that all the leaves around her were vibrating. She wriggled slowly up to Bartholomew and stood in front of him. He folded some of his legs and glared at her.

'It is unscientifical to believe that the fruit will never run out,' he said. 'Everything runs out in the end, and unless you get your own while stocks last, you'll end up with nothing. You'll starve, and then you'll disappear.'

'Disappear?' said Suzie, gazing up at him and wondering what he meant.

He laughed, but it wasn't a friendly laugh. 'Yes, and the smallest will disappear first. Gone. That's where you'll be. Whoomph! It will be metamorphosophistication for you.'

'What's meta ... metamorph ... what's that?' asked Suzie, in a very small voice.

'Oh, you have to be educated like me to use words like metamorphosophistication,' said Bartholomew. 'You can just call it the Terrible Darkness.' He laughed an ugly laugh and narrowed his eyes.

Wilma Wiggle came wiggling up to stand beside Suzie.

'What's the Terrible Darkness?' she asked, looking Bartholomew straight in the eye. She had decided that she didn't like this new caterpillar at all, and she wanted to defend Suzie.

Bartholomew's expression changed. He seemed almost friendly as he looked at Wilma, although there was still a strange glint in his eyes.

'Hello gorgeous,' he said. 'I can tell this is a very uneducated colony of caterpillars living on this tree. Normally I mix with intelligentual creatures, but I don't mind spending a bit of time with you, imparting my great wisdom to you.' He sat down and lowered his voice so that the caterpillars had to come closer to hear what he was saying.

'The Terrible Darkness is the worst thing there is,' he said in a low, threatening voice. 'It's so terrifying that nobody should even speak of it except in a whisper.' He looked round at all the caterpillar faces which were reflecting fear for the first time. 'The Terrible Darkness is what happens to stupid caterpillars who don't know how to protect themselves. Their bodies disappear slowly inside a cocoon, and in the cocoon there's no light, no air, no food, no nothing. It's the end of everything. No more wriggling about the tree! No more talking to your friends! No more sunshine! It's the end! Wham!' He clapped his feet together so hard that all his suckers stuck together, but the caterpillars were much too frightened to laugh as they watched him trying to pull them apart.

They looked at each other and on each face there was the same mixture of sadness and terror. They knew that Bartholomew must be telling the truth, for had not all the caterpillars who had ever lived on the tree eventually turned into cocoons? The caterpillars had never wondered why that happened. They had never asked themselves what life was like inside a cocoon, or what became of the caterpillars afterwards. They had just accepted it as a natural part of a caterpillar's life. But now, listening to Bartholomew, they knew that they had been foolish. He was right. It must be truly terrible to become a cocoon.

'Can't we do anything to avoid the Terrible Darkness?' asked Sybil Slow, who was old and knew that she would become a cocoon very soon.

'There is one thing,' said Bartholomew, rippling his green body. 'You must become as fat as me. You must eat and eat and eat, and then you will be too fat to fit inside a cocoon. Nobody has ever heard of a fat caterpillar becoming a cocoon.'

Only Lionel Loop-a-Lot looked vaguely comforted by this piece of information. Poor Wilma Wiggle turned a paler shade of green and looked anxiously down at her long thin body.

They had a meeting among themselves and decided that what Bartholomew had said made sense, so they divided the tree up among themselves and stuck signs on all the apples saying 'No Trespassers!', and they ate, and ate, and ate.

Soon they were all so fat that they could hardly move. And because they were all eating so much, the fruit was beginning to run out.

'You see,' said Bartholomew. 'I told you the fruit would run out one day. Aren't you glad you listened to me?'

They nodded meekly, although in fact there was very little to be glad about.

Some of the caterpillars finished their fruit before the others, and then the only way they could stay alive was to attack the others and steal the fruit that was left. Soon, a terrible war was being waged on the tree, but despite all their efforts, one by one the older caterpillars were still turning into cocoons. Sybil had eaten so much that she had become almost round, but even so, they woke up one morning to find her hanging from a leaf in a yellow silk cocoon.

'Why are we turning into cocoons when we've been eating so much?' they asked Bartholomew.

'Because you're not fat enough,' he said, puffing out his cheeks and looking smug.

So they fought all the more, and they ate all the more, until there was nothing left on the tree but a few ragged leaves and small, bitter green apples, and there were cocoons hanging from every branch.

One day, another stranger came to live on the tree. His name was Bert and he wasn't nearly as impressive as Bartholomew. He was an ordinary brown caterpillar with no bright spots or yellow suckers to brighten up his appearance. But when Bert laughed, it was as

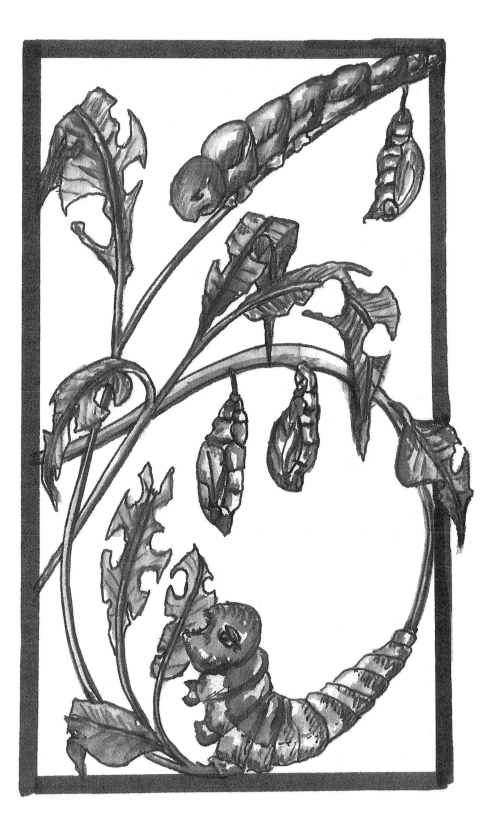

if the whole tree was wrapped in a warm glow so that even the shrivelled leaves and unripe fruit looked better. The caterpillars tried to explain to Bert that he ought to claim himself some fruit before it all ran out, but Bert said he had never owned anything in his life, and he didn't intend to start now.

'But what will you eat?' asked Suzie.

Bert smiled at Suzie. 'I would like to share your fruit, Suzie,' he said.

Suzie looked at her tiny, chewed up apple and thought there was hardly enough left for another meal for her. Then she looked at Bert's kind face and gentle smile, and she nodded shyly. 'There's not much,' she said, 'but we'll share what's left.'

Bert looked at Suzie's apple. 'There's enough there for a party,' he said. 'We're going to have the best party there has ever been. Go and call the caterpillars, Suzie. Tell them to come and celebrate with us.'

Bartholomew, who somehow always ended up with the biggest apple on the tree, looked down from his fruit and shook his head. 'He is mad,' he said to Suzie. 'He is completely and utterably nuts. Bonkers. Off his rocker. Suffering from a dreadful case of instabilanity, if you ask me.'

Suzie had to admit, it didn't seem like a very sensible suggestion to have a party, when there was hardly anything to eat and very little to celebrate. But there was something about Bert which made her trust him, so she called the other caterpillars and they all gathered around Bert. He broke off a piece of Suzie's apple and handed it to Wilma Wiggle, then another which he gave to Sebastian Squirm, then another which he gave to Lionel Loop-a-Lot. The caterpillars watched in amazement, for every time Bert broke a piece off, the apple grew, so that the more he gave, the more there was to give until the caterpillars had eaten their fill, and still the apple looked round and juicy and whole.

'Hmph,' said Bartholomew, who had not condescended to join in the feast. 'That's a cheap trick. Anyone can do that.'

Wilma Wiggle turned to face him. 'If anyone can do it, why didn't you do it when you knew we were all hungry and fighting over the last few mouthfuls of food?'

Bert shrugged. 'I've told you, I'm an intellectuable caterpillar. I don't go round performing party tricks to entertain the crowds.'

For a while, there was great happiness on the tree. The caterpillars went back to their old way of life, sharing what they had with one another, no longer fighting among themselves. Slowly, the tree began to recover. The fruit ripened and fresh green leaves appeared. Bert entertained them with stories and songs, and parties for every occasion because Bert loved celebrations. Then one day, a great sadness descended over the tree. Wilma Wiggle had become a cocoon.

'You see,' said Bartholomew, laughing at

their sad faces. 'She was too thin, that was her trouble. If she'd taken my advice, this would never have happened. She'd have been with you now, instead of being trapped in the Terrible Darkness.'

The caterpillars went to Bert and told him what had happened to Wilma Wiggle.

'But why do you look so sad? You ought to be celebrating for her,' said Bert.

They wondered if Bartholomew was right. Maybe Bert really was mad. They carefully explained to him about the Terrible Darkness.

'Oh,' said Bert, smiling broadly. 'I don't call it the Terrible Darkness. I call it the Wonderful Awakening.'

He gathered them round himself, and with the sun glinting on the fruit and shimmering on the leaves, he told them the most wonderful story that had ever been told.

'Look up,' he said. 'What do you see?'

The caterpillars looked up. 'We see the sky,' they said.

'Do you ever wonder what it would be like to be able to fly, so that you could leave your tree and dance with the birds?'

The caterpillars looked at each other and laughed, for not even in their wildest dreams could they imagine these wriggly bodies flying like birds.

'Look around you,' said Bert. 'This tree grows in a beautiful garden where there are many trees and flowers and fruits. Can you imagine rising with the sun in the morning and sipping nectar from all the flowers in the garden, being free to go wherever you choose and settle on any tree which tempts you?'

The caterpillars shook their heads. None of them had ever wondered what it was like to live anywhere else but on their tree.

'You weren't made to live on the tree forever. You really belong up there.' He pointed to the distant blue sky. 'One day, the whole garden will be your home. All of you will become cocoons and fall asleep, and when you wake up you will have wings which will allow you to leave the tree and to explore all the beauty around you. It is the most wonderful thing that can happen to a caterpillar, and that is why it's called the Wonderful Awakening. What you call the Terrible Darkness seems frightening I know, but if you didn't go through that, you would never become butterflies.'

He spoke with such conviction that the caterpillars believed him, and they went to tell Bartholomew the good news.

'It's alright,' they said. 'We are no longer afraid of the Terrible Darkness. It isn't an end at all, it's the beginning of a wonderful new life.' Then they repeated the story which Bert had told them.

Bartholomew laughed and laughed. 'Look at you!' he said. 'Where are these wings then? Why, everybody knows that caterpillars can't even jump, let alone fly! You're even more stupid than I thought! You have been completely deludicated by that brown grub that dares to call himself a caterpillar. I ask you! Have you ever seen such a nondescriptable creature. If you want to see what a caterpillar should look like, well, look at me.'

With that, he puffed out his body and flexed his yellow suckers, then he laughed. 'I'll tell you what,' he said. 'Ask him for proof. Tell Bert to prove that there's such a thing as butterflies. It's the most incredulable story I ever heard. I can prove to you that the Terrible Darkness exists. Look at what happened to Wilma Wiggle and Sybil Slow. But can Bert prove that the Wonderful Awakening exists?'

The caterpillars went back to Bert, and Lionel Loop-a-Lot spoke on behalf of all of them. 'The thing is, Bert, we really want to believe you, but we have no proof. How do we know that butterflies exist?'

'If I proved to you that butterflies exist, would you believe me? Would you stop being afraid?' asked Bert.

'Of course we would,' they all said.

That night, Bert told them stories and sang songs with them and fed them with the best fruit they had ever tasted, but there was a sadness about him as if he knew something which they did not know. He said goodbye to them one by one as they wriggled away to find a warm corner to sleep in.

The next morning, when Suzie went to visit Bert, he had disappeared. In his place was a small white cocoon, hanging forlornly from a branch of the tree.

She went crying to the other caterpillars to tell them the news.

'It's the Terrible Darkness,' she said. 'Bert has disappeared into the Terrible Darkness.'

Bartholomew smiled and licked his lips. 'Told you so,' he said.

In vain, they waited for something to happen, but Bert's cocoon didn't move. It didn't grow wings and fly up to dance with the birds. It just hung from the tree and did nothing.

The caterpillars went sadly back to their branches. Some of them put signs up and claimed their own fruit, but some remembered how Bert had taught them to share again, and they went on sharing. Sometimes they sat and cried beside Bert's cocoon, because they had grown to love him and they missed him.

Then one day, when Suzie went to Bert's cocoon, a miracle had happened. It was empty. Bert was no longer there. She ran back to tell the others what she had seen.

'It's true,' she said. 'The Wonderful Awakening has happened! Bert isn't in his cocoon!'

The caterpillars rushed to Bert's cocoon, and they saw that Suzie was right. The cocoon was empty.

Then they felt a gentle breeze fanning the air, and the most beautiful creature in the world alighted on the cocoon. It had wings which reflected all the colours of the garden, and long graceful legs and curving antennae.

'Now do you believe me?' the creature asked,

and the caterpillars recognised the voice and the loving glow in his eyes.

Then they watched as Bert's wings trembled into life and he rose high, high above their heads and disappeared into the sky to dance with the birds.

I wish I could say that everything was fine after that on the caterpillar tree, but from that day to this there have been some amazing arguments among the caterpillars.

Some refuse to believe in butterflies at all. They keep eating and fighting over the fruit, because what Bartholomew said must be true. He never has become a cocoon and he really is terribly, terribly fat.

Some believe in butterflies, but can't agree what butterflies look like. They argue and argue about whether butterflies have blue wings or red, green bodies or brown. The caterpillars who don't believe in butterflies laugh at them for being so stupid.

But there are a few caterpillars who know the truth. They live together in peace and happiness, sharing the fruit, remembering the stories which Bert told them, trying to help the others on the tree to be happy. They know that butterflies exist because they don't keep their eyes fixed on the tree all the time. Sometimes they take time to lie on their backs to look up at the sky, and they see that the sky shimmers with thousands and thousands of butterflies wings – some blue, some red, some with colours as subtle and changing as the

sunset. And that's not all. They've also noticed something which none of the other caterpillars have noticed – all the cocoons which
hang from the tree are empty.

12

A grandfather's story

*This poem offers a new look at a very old story.
It tells the story of Creation from the beginning
to the end of time, as it is experienced by
the animals on an African plain.*

In Africa
when the breezes sigh,
when the birds of the night
stretch their wings and fly,
when the moon looks down on the rolling
   plains,
and touches the tips of the hills with her
   beams,
Siphiwe sleeps
and Siphiwe dreams.

She dreams of a time when Africa lies
at peace beneath the gentle skies.
The rain falls softly, washing away
the droughts and the hunger of yesterday.
The animals browse
through the whispering grass,
and how, she asks,
did this come to pass?

From another age
and another place,
her grandfather visits
the land of her dreams.

The old man sits by a smouldering fire.
His voice drifts over the heads of his folk.

Siphiwe squats on the ground at his feet,
and sees his words
making pictures
in the smoke.

Once long ago,
there was peace in the world.
All the animals lived in a beautiful place,
where grazing was good
and their Ruler was God.

But the snake was a creature
of darkness and lies,
who wriggled and writhed
in the dirt and the slime,
and decided one day
to destroy
Paradise.

Look at you,
he said to the beasts.
What fools you are,
to live as you do.
If you were wise and knew
what I do,
you would ask for a king
who would rule over you,
and would help you to do
the most wonderful things.
Then you could all become
like kings.
But God is our King,
all the animals cried.

And where is this King?
the Serpent replied.

The creatures looked up to the African sky,
to the clouds and the sun and the
    shimmering light,
He is there,
He is high,
He is dazzling and bright.
Our King dwells
in the highest height.

The Serpent lifted his terrible head,
and he scornfully said
to the animal world,
He's not really there,
but you're all so scared
that you do not dare
to choose for yourselves
a better king.
A king who is here,
not high up there.
A king of the Earth,
a king of worth,
who will lend you his might
and will help you to fight
every beast and foe
that stands in your way,
so that all that you see,
in the sky and below,
will be yours one day.
The animals called to their King above,
reveal yourself in your glory and love.

But their King remained silent,
hidden from sight.

They argued far into the dark dark night
and finally said,
the Serpent is right.
Our King doesn't care,
he's not even there.
Let us choose from ourselves
a better King.

Far above where the fish eagle flies,
higher than anything else in the skies,
a voice was heard.
It was asking why
they no longer believed,
though their King was revealed
in the world all around.
In the sun and the rains,
in the rivers and plains.
The oceans and land
were the work of his hand.
All their joy,
all their love,
came from Heaven above.
In everything
they could see their King.

There was no other King but he,
but if the animals chose to be free,
He would release them in love
and in pain.

No more would he send them the life-giving
    rain,
protect them,
caress them,
and constantly bless them.
As he let them go
he was softly saying,
I want you to know
that I love you still
and I always will.

The animals looked at each other with eyes
which no longer reflected his love.
They began to envy,
to hate and despise,
for all wanted power
and they could not agree
which creature should be
their king.

They fought in the glare of the African sun,
which was no longer gentle and mild.
The grass was scorched,
the rivers ran dry,
and the animals fell
one by one.
Until at last
the lion alone
stood proud and powerful and strong,
while the Serpent smiled
and looked on.
So the lion became the king of the beasts,
and the Serpent said it was right.

Here was a better king by far
than their distant unseen invisible King,
who was hidden in glory and light.

But such a King has never been seen.
From that day on,
all joy was gone
from Africa.

For thousands of years he hunted and
  prowled,
killing his subjects
and filling his kingdom with fear.

No more did the antelope browse in peace,
in the gentle, nurturing plains.
The young and the frail, the weak and the old
were preyed upon,
set upon,
brown eyes wide,
terrified.
All were victims
of their king.

The animals looked to the sky above,
sighing and crying
in their hopelessness
to the Unseen King,
who had reigned with love
and gentleness.

The Serpent saw their sorrow
and smiled.

But high in the heavens the infinite King
had seen the pain in the world below.
Quietly, one night, he said I will go
to my suffering world,
and then they will know
that I love them still,
and I always will.

But I will not rule them with tooth and with
    claw,
I will go to them as I really am.
Gentle and lowly, humble and poor,
I will live with them
as a spotless Lamb.

The Lamb came from Heaven
to live with the beasts,
and although he was helpless and small,
he taught them
and fed them
and tenderly led them.
He loved them and cared for them all.

They followed him gladly, wherever
        he went,
for he told them he had been sent
to bring them peace,
and love
from their King above,
who loved them still,
and always will.
His presence brought comfort and healing
from the fears

and the tears
and the sadness of living
with the king they had chosen,
until one day they asked,
Would you be our King
instead?

But the Serpent hissed
and said to the beasts,
What kind of king is this,
this little, helpless, foolish thing?
You have been deceived,
again!

The animals looked at the Lamb they had
loved,
and they had to admit it was true.
This Lamb really wasn't much of a king.
But did that matter?
After all,
power isn't everything.

Show them your might,
hissed the snake to the lion.
Roar and astound them,
bewitch and confound them,
for you are their king,
are you not?

With a terrible roar
the lion showed his power.
The animals trembled,
remembered,

and said,
we have no king but you.

They turned on the Lamb
with their talons and claws.
They drowned his voice,
with their barks
and their cries
and their calls.

The Serpent lay in the ground at their feet.
Kill him,
he said,
for the lion is your king.

They went to the lion,
and they said he must die,
this Lamb
who would claim to be King.

So the lion agreed,
and the sky turned black,
as the lion performed the terrible deed.

But the Lamb lay dying,
in his agony crying,
and he said I forgive you,
I love you still,
I always will.

What have we done?
the animals wailed,
when they saw

that the Lamb
had been slain.

One by one they acknowledged their King
and they wept
in their sadness and pain.

In vain
the Serpent smiled.

'Look at the lion,' he tried to persuade them.
With all of his cunning he tried to dissuade
   them
from calling the Lamb
their King.

But nothing the Serpent could say or do
could convince them ever again,
for now they knew
what had always been true,
that their King
was the Lamb
that was slain.

Even the lion bowed his head down low,
and with sorrow so great
that his heart might break,
he said now I know
he was truly our King.
What I have done is a terrible thing.
Can he really love me still?
Is it true he always will?

Far above
the Almighty saw
what his creatures had done
to the Lamb.
But he sighed on the earth
with a mighty breath,
and he raised the Lamb
and he called him home.
He seated his child upon his throne,
for he was the Lamb,
and the Lamb was his own.

He enfolded the Lamb
in his infinite love
and they washed the world
with their tears,
as one by one,
during two thousand years,
every creature knelt
and raised his head
and lifted his heart
and began to sing
a gentle, sorrowing, sighing hymn,
All Praise to our One and Only King.

High above all the things of the earth,
the Almighty said,
It is done.
Now is the time for the second birth,
when my creatures and I
will be one.
For I love them still,
and I always will.

He watered the land
with his nurturing rains.
All the mountains and valleys,
the deserts and plains
drank and rejoiced,
as the earth raised its voice,
to sing of the bright new day.

He gathered up
all the birds and the beasts
in arms of unending love.
He dried their tears
and he stilled their fears.
He said I am with you,
I'll never forsake you,
for I love you still
and I always will.

The lion lay down with the Lamb at
        his side,
the doors of Heaven were opened wide,
and peace was restored
beneath the moon,
the African moon.

It's over,
too soon, too soon.

Siphiwe comes back from the land of her
    dreams,
to the bright warm beams
of another day.

But the story goes on,
and when dreams come true,
it may happen to you.
An old man waits
by the glow of a fire,
inviting you to hear it too.
Will you come?